GATORS • MILD-MANNERED MICE • KINDHEARTED KOALAS • BENEFICEN
OUS HORSES • OUTGOING OWLS • MAGNANIMOUS MONKEYS • EAGER ELEPHANTS
S • PLEASANT PENGUINS • HOSPITABLE HOGS • CARIN ALLI
TRUSTWORTHY TURTLES • LOVABLE LEMURS • SAINTLY SNAILS HARMO
BENEVOLENT BUNNIES • FRIENDLY FROGS • SOCIABLE SNAKES • BEATIFI
ABLE ALLIGATORS • MILD-MANNERED MICE • KINDHEARTED KOALAS • BEN
HARMONIOUS HORSES • OUTGOING OWLS • MAGNANIMOUS MONKEYS • EA
S BEATIFIC BEETLES • PLEASANT PENGUINS • HOSPITABLE HOGS • CARIN
BENEFICENT BIRDS • TRUSTWORTHY TURTLES • LOVABLE LEMURS • SAINTL
ER ELEPHANTS • BENEVOLENT BUNNIES • FRIENDLY FROGS • SOCIABLE SNAKE
S • AMIABLE ALLIGATORS • MILD-MANNERED MICE • KINDHEARTED KOALAS
SNAILS • HARMONIOUS HORSES • OUTGOING OWLS • MAGNANIMOUS MON
LE SNAKES • BEATIFIC BEETLES • PLEASANT PENGUINS • HOSPITABLE HOGS
AS • BENEFICENT BIRDS • TRUSTWORTHY TURTLES • LOVABLE LEMURS • SAINTL
ER ELEPHANTS • BENEVOLENT BUNNIES • FRIENDLY FROGS • SOCIABLE SNAKES
AMIABLE ALLIGATORS • MILD-MANNERED MICE • KINDHEARTED KOALAS • B
• HARMONIOUS HORSES • OUTGOING OWLS • MAGNANIMOUS MONKEYS • EAGER
BEATIFIC BEETLES • PLEASANT PENGUINS • HOSPITABLE HOGS • CARING CATS
FICENT BIRDS • TRUSTWORTHY TURTLES • LOVABLE LEMURS • SAINTLY SNAILS
LEPHANTS • BENEVOLENT BUNNIES • FRIENDLY FROGS • SOCIABLE SNAKES
• AMIABLE ALLIGATORS • MILD-MANNERED MICE • KINDHEARTED KOALAS • B
S • HARMONIOUS HORSES • OUTGOING OWLS • MAGNANIMOUS MONKEYS • EAC
• BEATIFIC BEETLES • PLEASANT PENGUINS • HOSPITABLE HOGS • CARING
BENEFICENT BIRDS • TRUSTWORTHY TURTLES • LOVABLE LEMURS • SAINTLY
ER ELEPHANTS • BENEVOLENT BUNNIES • FRIENDLY FROGS • SOCIABLE SNAKES
• AMIABLE ALLIGATORS • MILD-MANNERED MICE • KINDHEARTED KOALAS • B
LILS • HARMONIOUS HORSES • OUTGOING OWLS • MAGNANIMOUS MONKEYS
ES • BEATIFIC BEETLES • PLEASANT PENGUINS • HOSPITABLE HOGS • CARIN
BENEFICENT BIRDS • TRUSTWORTHY TURTLES • LOVABLE LEMURS • SAINTLY
ER ELEPHANTS • BENEVOLENT BUNNIES • FRIENDLY FROGS • SOCIABLE SNAKES
• AMIABLE ALLIGATORS • MILD-MANNERED MICE • KINDHEARTED KOALAS
HARMONIOUS HORSES • OUTGOING OWLS • MAGNANIMOUS MONKEYS • EAGE

LEASANT PENGUINS • HOSPITABLE HOGS • CARING CATS • AMIABLE ALLIGATOR
MILD-MANNERED MICE • KINDHEARTED KOALAS • BENEFICENT BIRDS • TRUS
WORTHY TURTLES • LOVABLE LEMURS • SAINTLY SNAILS • HARMONIOUS HORSE
OUTGOING OWLS • MAGNANIMOUS MONKEYS • EAGER ELEPHANTS • BENEVOLE
BUNNIES • FRIENDLY FROGS • SOCIABLE SNAKES • BEATIFIC BEETLES • PLEA
NT PENGUINS • HOSPITABLE HOGS • CARING CATS • AMIABLE ALLIGATORS
MILD-MANNERED MICE • KINDHEARTED KOALAS • BENEFICENT BIRDS • TRUS
WORTHY TURTLES • LOVABLE LEMURS • SAINTLY SNAILS • HARMONIOUS HORS
OUTGOING OWLS • MAGNANIMOUS MONKEYS • EAGER ELEPHANTS • BENEVOLE
BUNNIES • FRIENDLY FROGS • SOCIABLE SNAKES • BEATIFIC BEETLES • PLEA
ANT PENGUINS • HOSPITABLE HOGS • CARING CATS • AMIABLE ALLIGATORS
MILD-MANNERED MICE • KINDHEARTED KOALAS • BENEFICENT BIRDS • TRU
WORTHY TURTLES • LOVABLE LEMURS • SAINTLY SNAILS • HARMONIOUS HORS
OUTGOING OWLS • MAGNANIMOUS MONKEYS • EAGER ELEPHANTS • BENEVOLE
BUNNIES • FRIENDLY FROGS • SOCIABLE SNAKES • BEATIFIC BEETLES • PLEA
ANT PENGUINS • HOSPITABLE HOGS • CARING CATS • AMIABLE ALLIGATORS
MILD-MANNERED MICE • KINDHEARTED KOALAS • BENEFICENT BIRDS • TRU
WORTHY TURTLES • LOVABLE LEMURS • SAINTLY SNAILS • HARMONIOUS HORS
OUTGOING OWLS • MAGNANIMOUS MONKEYS • EAGER ELEPHANTS • BENEVOLE
BUNNIES • FRIENDLY FROGS • SOCIABLE SNAKES • BEATIFIC BEETLES • PLEA
ANT PENGUINS • HOSPITABLE HOGS • CARING CATS • AMIABLE ALLIGATORS
MILD-MANNERED MICE • KINDHEARTED KOALAS • BENEFICENT BIRDS • TRU
WORTHY TURTLES • LOVABLE LEMURS • SAINTLY SNAILS • HARMONIOUS HORS
OUTGOING OWLS • MAGNANIMOUS MONKEYS • EAGER ELEPHANTS • BENEVOLE
BUNNIES • FRIENDLY FROGS • SOCIABLE SNAKES • BEATIFIC BEETLES • PLE
ANT PENGUINS • HOSPITABLE HOGS • CARING CATS • AMIABLE ALLIGATORS
MILD-MANNERED MICE • KINDHEARTED KOALAS • BENEFICENT BIRDS • TRU
WORTHY TURTLES • LOVABLE LEMURS • SAINTLY SNAILS • HARMONIOUS HORS
OUTGOING OWLS • MAGNANIMOUS MONKEYS • EAGER ELEPHANTS • BENEVOLE
BUNNIES • FRIENDLY FROGS • SOCIABLE SNAKES • BEATIFIC BEETLES • PLE
ANT PENGUINS • HOSPITABLE HOGS • CARING CATS • AMIABLE ALLIGATORS
MILD-MANNERED MICE • KINDHEARTED KOALAS • BENEFICENT BIRDS •

The NICE Book

David Ezra Stein

G. P. PUTNAM'S SONS

CUDDLE

nestle

nuzzle

Don't tickle

... well, maybe a little.

**LOVE WAS
MEANT TO BE
PASSED ON.**

SCRATCH

PAT

...BUT I'M NOT THE FLEA.

When you get in a snit,

DON'T HIT–

say how you feel.

Take time

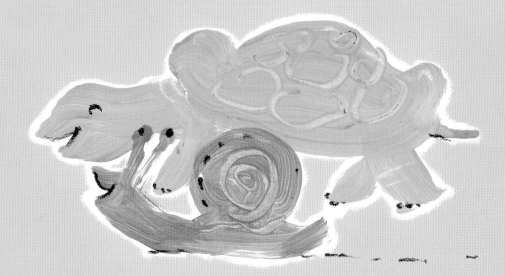

get away

hear what someone has to say.

SING A SONG TO SOMEONE.

OR SING TO YOURSELF.

LOOK

...but don't stare.

If you have more than you need,

SHARE.

LOOK AFTER SOMEONE LITTLE.

WE'RE ALL LITTLE.

Say hello.

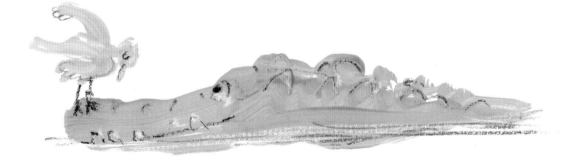

BREAK THE ICE.

And don't forget,

BE NICE!

To STANLEY and BASTA, those nice animals—D. E. S.

G. P. PUTNAM'S SONS
A division of Penguin Young Readers Group.
Published by The Penguin Group.
Penguin Group (USA) Inc., 375 Hudson Street, New York, NY 10014, U.S.A.
Penguin Group (Canada), 90 Eglinton Avenue East, Suite 700, Toronto, Ontario M4P 2Y3, Canada (a division of Pearson Penguin Canada Inc.).
Penguin Books Ltd, 80 Strand, London WC2R 0RL, England.
Penguin Ireland, 25 St. Stephen's Green, Dublin 2, Ireland (a division of Penguin Books Ltd.).
Penguin Group (Australia), 250 Camberwell Road, Camberwell, Victoria 3124, Australia (a division of Pearson Australia Group Pty Ltd).
Penguin Books India Pvt Ltd, 11 Community Centre, Panchsheel Park, New Delhi - 110 017, India.
Penguin Group (NZ), 67 Apollo Drive, Rosedale, North Shore 0632, New Zealand (a division of Pearson New Zealand Ltd).
Penguin Books (South Africa) (Pty) Ltd, 24 Sturdee Avenue, Rosebank, Johannesburg 2196, South Africa.
Penguin Books Ltd, Registered Offices: 80 Strand, London WC2R 0RL, England.

Design by David Ezra Stein and Katrina Damkoehler. Text set in Quadrille 2, Moulin Rouge, Madrone STD, Antique 3, Square Dance, Extravaganza, and Hearst Italic.
The art was created using acrylic paint, inks, china marker, and digital.

Library of Congress Cataloging-in-Publication Data
Stein, David Ezra.
The nice book / David Ezra Stein.   p. cm.
Summary: Monkeys, mice, snakes, cats, and many other animals demonstrate how to act towards others.
[1. Animals—Fiction. 2. Behavior—Fiction.] I. Title.
PZ7.S8179Ho 2008   [E]—dc22   2007043163

ISBN 978-0-399-25050-7
10 9 8 7 6 5 4 3 2 1

EASANT PENGUINS • HOSPITABLE HOGS • CARING CATS • AMIABLE ALLIGATORS
MILD-MANNERED MICE • KINDHEARTED KOALAS • BENEFICENT BIRDS • TRUS
RTHY TURTLES • LOVABLE LEMURS • SAINTLY SNAILS • HARMONIOUS HORSE
OUTGOING OWLS • MAGNANIMOUS MONKEYS • EAGER ELEPHANTS • BENEVOLEN
NNIES • FRIENDLY FROGS • SOCIABLE SNAKES • BEATIFIC BEETLES • PLEASAN
NGUINS • HOSPITABLE HOGS • CARING CATS • AMIABLE ALLIGATORS • MILD
NNERED MICE • KINDHEARTED KOALAS • BENEFICENT BIRDS • TRUSTWO
Y TURTLES • LOVABLE LEMURS • SAINTLY SNAILS • HARMONIOUS HORSES
TGOING OWLS • MAGNANIMOUS MONKEYS • EAGER ELEPHANTS • BENEVOLEN
UNNIES • FRIENDLY FROGS • SOCIABLE SNAKES • BEATIFIC BEETLES • PLEAS
T PENGUINS • HOSPITABLE HOGS • CARING CATS • AMIABLE ALLIGATORS •
LD-MANNERED MICE • KINDHEARTED KOALAS • BENEFICENT BIRDS • TRUS
ORTHY TURTLES • LOVABLE LEMURS • SAINTLY SNAILS • HARMONIOUS HORSE
OUTGOING OWLS • MAGNANIMOUS MONKEYS • EAGER ELEPHANTS • BENEVOLEN
UNNIES • FRIENDLY FROGS • SOCIABLE SNAKES • BEATIFIC BEETLES • PLEAS
T PENGUINS • HOSPITABLE HOGS • CARING CATS • AMIABLE ALLIGATORS •
LD-MANNERED MICE • KINDHEARTED KOALAS • BENEFICENT BIRDS • TRUS
ORTHY TURTLES • LOVABLE LEMURS • SAINTLY SNAILS • HARMONIOUS HORSE
OUTGOING OWLS • MAGNANIMOUS MONKEYS • EAGER ELEPHANTS • BENEVOLEN
UNNIES • FRIENDLY FROGS • SOCIABLE SNAKES • BEATIFIC BEETLES • PLEAS
T PENGUINS • HOSPITABLE HOGS • CARING CATS • AMIABLE ALLIGATORS •
LD-MANNERED MICE • KINDHEARTED KOALAS • BENEFICENT BIRDS • TRUS
ORTHY TURTLES • LOVABLE LEMURS • SAINTLY SNAILS • HARMONIOUS HORSES
OUTGOING OWLS • MAGNANIMOUS MONKEYS • EAGER ELEPHANTS • BENEVOLEN
UNNIES • FRIENDLY FROGS • SOCIABLE SNAKES • BEATIFIC BEETLES • PLEAS
T PENGUINS • HOSPITABLE HOGS • CARING CATS • AMIABLE ALLIGATORS
LD-MANNERED MICE • KINDHEARTED KOALAS • BENEFICENT BIRDS • TRUS
ORTHY TURTLES • LOVABLE LEMURS • SAINTLY SNAILS • HARMONIOUS HORSES
OUTGOING OWLS • MAGNANIMOUS MONKEYS • EAGER ELEPHANTS • BENEVOLEN
NNIES • FRIENDLY FROGS • SOCIABLE SNAKES • BEATIFIC BEETLES • PLEA
T PENGUINS • HOSPITABLE HOGS • CARING CATS • AMIABLE ALLIGATORS
LD-MANNERED MICE • KINDHEARTED KOALAS • BENEFICENT BIRDS • TRUS

PLEASANT PENGUINS • HOSPITABLE HOGS • CARING CATS • AMIABLE A
BIRDS • TRUSTWORTHY TURTLES • LOVABLE LEMURS • SAINTLY SNAILS • HARMO
BENEVOLENT BUNNIES • FRIENDLY FROGS • SOCIABLE SNAKES • BEATIFIC BEE
ATORS • MILD-MANNERED MICE • KINDHEARTED KOALAS • ENT BIR
OUS HORSES • OUTGOING OWLS • MAGNANIMOUS MONKEYS • EAGER ELEPHAN
BEETLES • PLEASANT PENGUINS • HOSPITABLE HOGS • CARING CATS • A
FICENT BIRDS • TRUSTWORTHY TURTLES • LOVABLE LEMURS • SAINTLY SNA
ER ELEPHANTS • BENEVOLENT BUNNIES • FRIENDLY FROGS • SOCIABLE SNA
CATS • AMIABLE ALLIGATORS • MILD-MANNERED MICE • KINDHEARTED KOALA
SNAILS • HARMONIOUS HORSES • OUTGOING OWLS • MAGNANIMOUS MONKEYS •
BEATIFIC BEETLES • PLEASANT PENGUINS • HOSPITABLE HOGS • CARING
BENEFICENT BIRDS • TRUSTWORTHY TURTLES • LOVABLE LEMURS • SAIN
KEYS • EAGER ELEPHANTS • BENEVOLENT BUNNIES • FRIENDLY FROGS • SOCI
CARING CATS • AMIABLE ALLIGATORS • MILD-MANNERED MICE • KINDHEARTED KO
SNAILS • HARMONIOUS HORSES • OUTGOING OWLS • MAGNANIMOUS MONKEYS •
BEATIFIC BEETLES • PLEASANT PENGUINS • HOSPITABLE HOGS • CARING CA
NEFICENT BIRDS • TRUSTWORTHY TURTLES • LOVABLE LEMURS • SAINTLY SNA
ELEPHANTS • BENEVOLENT BUNNIES • FRIENDLY FROGS • SOCIABLE SNAKES •
AMIABLE ALLIGATORS • MILD-MANNERED MICE • KINDHEARTED KOALAS • BE
HARMONIOUS HORSES • OUTGOING OWLS • MAGNANIMOUS MONKEYS • EAGER
BEATIFIC BEETLES • PLEASANT PENGUINS • HOSPITABLE HOGS • CARING CAT
NEFICENT BIRDS • TRUSTWORTHY TURTLES • LOVABLE LEMURS • SAINTLY SN
ER ELEPHANTS • BENEVOLENT BUNNIES • FRIENDLY FROGS • SOCIABLE SNA
CATS • AMIABLE ALLIGATORS • MILD-MANNERED MICE • KINDHEARTED KOALAS
SNAILS • HARMONIOUS HORSES • OUTGOING OWLS • MAGNANIMOUS MONKEYS •
BEATIFIC BEETLES • PLEASANT PENGUINS • HOSPITABLE HOGS • CARING CA
NEFICENT BIRDS • TRUSTWORTHY TURTLES • LOVABLE LEMURS • SAINTLY
EAGER ELEPHANTS • BENEVOLENT BUNNIES • FRIENDLY FROGS • SOCIABLE SN
CATS • AMIABLE ALLIGAT KINDHEARTED KOALA
SNAILS • HARMONIOUS HO ANIMOUS MONKEYS •
BEATIFIC BEETLES • PLEASANT PENGUINS • HOSPITABLE HOGS • CARING
NEFICENT BIRDS • TRUSTWORTHY TURTLES • LOVABLE LEMURS • SAINTLY SN